# Wise Owl's
# TIME BOOK

by Jane Belk Moncure
illustrated by Helen Endres
created by Child's World

 CHILDRENS PRESS, CHICAGO

**Library of Congress Cataloging in Publication Data**

Moncure, Jane Belk.
  Wise Owl's time book.

  (Wise Owl plus)
  SUMMARY: The little owls give Wise Owl a
clock for his birthday, and they all practice
moving the hands to show the hours of the day.
  [1. Time — Fiction.      2. Clocks — Fiction.
3. Owls — Fiction]      I. Endres, Helen, ill.
II. Title.
PZ7.M739Wj              [E]              81-38546
ISBN 0-516-06566-1                       AACR2

Wise Owl was late again. He was always late.

Today was Wise Owl's birthday. And he was late to his own birthday dinner.

"We did not wait for you," said Mrs. Owl from the kitchen.

Wise Owl sat at the table all alone. His dinner was cold. The room was dark.

"What an awful birthday," he said.

The lights flashed on.

"Surprise!" yelled four small owls as they hopped out from under the table.

"Happy Birthday!" they shouted.

The owlets put a HUGE box on the table.

"Guess what it is," begged Little Owl.

"Open it!" cried Baby Owl.

Wise Owl pulled out . . . a face! It had
numbers on it. "It must be a clock," he said. "A
BIG clock!"

"Just what you need for the office," said Mrs.
Owl. "Now you will know when to come home!"

"And you can tell when it is time to play ball," said Big Brother Owl.

"And when it is time to go fishing," said Middle Brother Owl.

"And when it is time to play with me," said Little Owl.

"Yes, I can," said Wise Owl. "But being on time will take a little practice."

"Practice!" shouted Big Brother Owl. "It is time for football practice."

"Let's go," said Middle Brother Owl.

"It's time for Baby Owl's bath," said Mrs. Owl. "Why don't you and Little Owl put the clock together?" she said to Wise Owl.

Wise Owl put the clock's face on the floor.

"I can count around the clock," said Little Owl.

"Let's see you do it," said Wise Owl.

Little Owl counted, "1, 2, 3, 4, 5, 6, 7, 8, 9, 10, 11, 12."

"Very good," said Wise Owl. "Tick-tock, tick-tock. There are twelve hours around the clock!"

"I can see the twelve hours around the clock,"
said Little Owl. "But how do you know which hour
is which?"

Wise Owl picked up a short, pointed piece of the clock.

"This is the short hand," he said. "It points to the hour."

Wise Owl put the short hand on the clock's face. It pointed to the 7.

"Is it 7 o'clock?" asked Little Owl.

"Yes," said Wise Owl. "The short hand is pointing to 7 of the clock."

Next Wise Owl picked up a long, pointed piece of the clock.

"This is the long hand," he said. "It points to the minutes in each hour."

Wise Owl put the long hand on the clock's face. It pointed to the 12. "Each hour starts when the long hand points straight up to the 12."

"That's easy," said Little Owl.

7:00

"We'll see," said Wise Owl. "We will play 'Round the Clock.

"I will set the clock at different hours," he said. "You tell me what you do during those hours. Start with the morning. What do you do at 7 in the morning?"

"I hop out of bed. I get dressed. And I eat breakfast!" said Little Owl.

8:00

"All the time the long hand moves around," said Wise Owl. "And the short hand moves up to the 8.

"Tick-tock, 8 o'clock. What do you do at 8 o'clock?" he asked.

"I ride on the school bus with my friends," said Little Owl.

"All the time the long hand moves around," said Wise Owl. "And the short hand moves up to . . ."

9:00

"...to 9!" said Little Owl. "At 9 o'clock we are working at school."

"How about 10 o'clock?" asked Wise Owl.

"That's easy. At 10 o'clock we have recess!" said Little Owl.

10:00

11:00

"At 11 o'clock on Fridays we go to the library."

"Good," said Wise Owl. He moved the short hand up to the 11.

12:00

"I know what time it is when both hands point to the 12," said Little Owl.

"What time is it?" Wise Owl winked.

"It is 12 o'clock! Time for lunch!" screeched Little Owl. "But, we have only half an hour for lunch."

"Let me show you what half of an hour looks like," said Wise Owl. "There are five minutes from one numeral to the next."

Wise Owl pushed the long hand around. He counted by fives. "Five, ten, fifteen, twenty, twenty-five, thirty. It is thirty minutes past the 12 — 12:30," said Wise Owl.

"We are almost done," said Wise Owl. "Just a coat of paint."

"Let's play the game some more," said Little Owl.

"All right. What do you do at 2:30?" Wise Owl asked.

"At 2:30, school is out," Little Owl answered. "I come home and play ball!

2:30

"Sometimes I play until 5:30.

5:30

"And at 6:30 we eat dinner," he said.

"If I am not late," said Wise Owl.

6:30

"Now I think you can tell the hours and half hours all around the clock," said Wise Owl.

"Maybe," said Little Owl. "But what about the times in between?"

"That takes more practice," answered Wise Owl. "Tomorrow we will take the clock to the office. I'll teach you more about minutes then."

Mrs. Owl came back. "It's late!" she said. "Do you know it is 8 o'clock?"

Wise Owl put the short hand on the 8. Then he put the long hand on the 12.

"BONG! BONG! BONG! BONG! BONG! BONG! BONG! BONG!" chimed the clock.

"This is the best birthday gift ever!" said Wise Owl.

Just then Big Brother and Middle Brother Owl rushed in.

"Are we too late?" they asked.

"Too late for what?" asked Wise Owl.

"Come to the table," said Mrs. Owl to Wise Owl. "Close your eyes."

Then Mrs. Owl brought in a birthday cake. It was shaped like a clock. And it had twelve candles on it, one for each hour around the clock.

"Why did you put twelve candles on Papa's cake? He's older than that," said Big Brother Owl.

"Because that's the way I like it," said Wise Owl.
"I never tell my age." He blew out the candles.

"Happy Birthday!" sang the owls.

And it had been a happy birthday.

# A Wise Owl Plus

Later, Little Owl learned about the minutes.

"There are 60 minutes in one hour," said Wise Owl. "The long hand moves around one minute at a time. Every time it points to a numeral, five minutes have gone by."

Wise Owl put both hands on the 12. Then he moved the long hand to the 1. As he moved it, he counted, "One, two, three, four, five minutes. Five minutes after 12."

Little Owl made a clock. He wanted to practice telling time.

You can make a practice clock, too. Here's how:

1.  Number one to twelve around a large paper plate.

2.  Mark the minute lines.

3.  Punch a hole in the center of the plate.

4.  Cut out a short hand and a long hand. (Use heavy black construction paper.)

5.  Attach the hands to the plate with a gold brad fastener.

6.  Turn the hands to practice the times on the clock's face. Match the times below.

7.  Read your clock.